J.A. CARLESS
1990.

KU-175-598

Stories for Summer

Also available in Beaver
STORIES FOR CHRISTMAS

Alf Prøysen

Stories for Summer

Illustrated by
Kari Grossman

Translated by
Patricia Crampton and Marianne Helweg

BEAVER BOOKS

A Beaver Book
Published by Arrow Books Limited
20 Vauxhall Bridge Road, London SW1V 2SA
An imprint of Random Century Group

London Melbourne Sydney Auckland
Johannesburg and agencies throughout the world

First published in Great Britain in 1989 by Hutchinson Children's Books

Beaver edition 1990

Copyright © Tiden Norsk Forlag 1987
English translation Copyright © Century Hutchinson Ltd 1989

This book is sold subject to the condition that
it shall not, by way of trade or otherwise, be lent,
resold, hired out, or otherwise circulated without the
publisher's prior consent in any form of binding or cover
other than that in which it is published and without a
similar condition including this condition being imposed
on the subsequent purchaser.

Printed and bound in Belgium
by Proost International Book Production

ISBN 0 09 969050 0

Contents

The kid that could count to ten

Once upon a time there was a little kid goat who had learned to count to ten.

When he came to a puddle he stood for a long time gazing at his reflection in the water and this is what happened next:

'One,' said the kid.

A calf walking by heard him as he stopped to munch some grass.

'What are you doing?' said the calf.

'I'm counting myself,' said the kid. 'Shall I count you too?'

'As long as it doesn't hurt,' said the calf.

'Of course it doesn't. Stand still and I'll count you.'

'No, I can't, my mother might not let me,' said the calf, and off he went. But the kid followed him.

'I am *one* and you are *two*, 1–2.'

'Moo-ther!' bellowed the calf, beginning to cry. Then the calf's mother came up, and she was the bell-cow of the farm.

'What are you mooing for?' said the bell-cow.

'The kid goat is counting me,' mooed the calf.

'What does that mean?' said the bell-cow.

'I'm counting,' said the kid. 'I have learned to count to ten. All I do is this: I am *one* and the calf is *two* and the cow is *three*, 1–2–3.'

'Oh, now he's counted you too!' mooed the calf.

When the bell-cow heard this she became terribly angry.

'I'll teach you to make a fool of my calf and me! Come on, my calf, let's have him!'

The bell-cow and the calf galloped straight towards the kid goat and he was so frightened that he sprang high in the air and shot away across the meadow with the cow and the calf behind him.

Some way off in his own field stood the ox, digging up large tussocks with his horns. Suddenly the kid and the calf and the cow came running by.

'Why are you chasing that little kid?' asked the ox.

'He's counting us,' mooed the calf.

'But we'll get him,' said the bell-cow.

'I am *one*, the calf is *two*, the cow is *three*, the ox is *four*, 1–2–3–4,' said the kid.

'Oh, now he's counted you too,' mooed the calf.

'Just let him try!' bellowed the ox, and he followed the others, all chasing after the kid goat.

Round the corner a horse was walking along,

cropping the grass, when all the animals came rushing past.

'What a speed you're going,' said the horse.

'We're going to get that kid,' said the cow.

'He's counting us,' mooed the calf.

'And he's not allowed to,' bellowed the ox.

'How does he do that?' said the horse.

'All I do is this,' said the kid. '*One* for me and *two* for the calf and *three* for the cow and *four* for the ox and *five* for the horse, 1–2–3–4–5.'

'Oh! Now he's counted you too!' mooed the calf.

'Just you wait, you little goat-for-nothing!' neighed the horse, and he began to gallop along the road with the others, after the kid goat.

In the pig sty lay a fat porker who had been asleep until the procession went rushing by.

'You're in a great hurry, all of you,' said the porker.

'We're going to get the kid,' said the cow.

'He's counting us!' mooed the calf.

'And he's not allowed to,' bellowed the ox.

'Just let him wait,' neighed the horse.

'What do you do when you count?' asked the porker.

'This is all I do,' said the kid. '*One* for me and *two* for the calf and *three* for the cow and *four* for the ox and *five* for the horse and *six* for the porker. 1–2–3–4–5–6.'

'Oh! Now he's counted you too,' mooed the calf.

'All the worse for him,' said the porker, and, breaking loose a plank of the sty with his snout, he set off after the others.

Up hill and down dale they went and through mud and mire until they came to a river. By the jetty lay a little boat, and on board the boat there were a cat and a dog and a sheep and a

11

cock. The cat was the cook, the sheep was the cabin-boy, the cock was the skipper and the dog was the pilot.

'Stop a minute, do!' crowed the cock, when he saw all the animals coming helter-skelter down the road. But it was too late. The kid braced

himself on the edge of the jetty and leaped on board with all the other animals behind him; the anchor chain snapped and the boat began to sail off towards the deepest part of the river. The cock was suddenly frightened.

'Come and help,' crowed the cock, 'the boat's sinking!'

Then all the animals were frightened, but the cock crowed again: 'Can any of you count?'

'I can!' said the kid.

'Then hurry up and count how many of us there are on board. The boat can only take ten passengers.'

'Hurry up and count!' cried the other animals.

And the kid goat counted.

'*One* for me, *two* for the calf, *three* for the cow, *four* for the ox, *five* for the horse, *six* for the porker, *seven* for the cat, *eight* for the dog, *nine* for the sheep and *ten* for the cock. 1–2–3–4–5–6–7–8–9–10.'

'Hurrah for the kid!' shouted all the animals, and off they sailed to the other bank, where they went ashore. But the kid goat stayed on as counting master, and every time the cock was taking passengers on board to ferry them across the river, the kid stood on the landing-stage and counted them – up to ten.

Mrs Pepperpot is taken for a witch

In the part of Norway where Mrs Pepperpot lives they always have a big firework party with a bonfire on Midsummer's Eve. Everybody – young and old, and the children too – stays up all night to dance and sing and enjoy themselves.

Only two people in that valley never go to the bonfire party, and they are Mrs Pepperpot and her husband. Do you know why?

Well, Midsummer's Eve happens to be Mr Pepperpot's birthday, so on that day he is the one who decides what they do, and he never likes going to parties where there are lots of people because he is always afraid that Mrs Pepperpot will suddenly shrink and leave him feeling so foolish that he does not know if he is coming or going.

But this year Mrs Pepperpot did go to the party and this is how it happened.

It began on the night before Midsummer's Eve. Mrs Pepperpot had been to the store and was walking slowly home with her basket on her arm. She was wondering how she could persuade her husband to go to the party and suddenly she had an idea.

Suppose I ask him if there is something he really wants for his birthday – then I could say I would give it to him if he promises to take me to the party.

As soon as she got inside the door she jumped on her husband's knee and gave him a smacking kiss on the tip of his ear.

'Dear, good little hubby,' she said, 'have you got a very special wish for your birthday tomorrow?'

'Have you got sunstroke or something?' gasped her husband. 'Where would you get the money from? Money runs through your fingers like water!'

'Oh, sometimes it does and sometimes it

15

doesn't,' said Mrs Pepperpot, sounding as sweet as sweet could be. 'There are such things as hens and such things as eggs and I have sold a few eggs and put by a tidy sum. Just tell me what you would like and the present will be on the table on Midsummer's Eve as sure as I'm sitting here,' she said.

Her husband laughed, but at the same time he thought he would set his wife a hard test.

'Well, if you have enough money to buy me that handsome pipe with the silver band from the store, I'll promise you something in return,' he said.

'Done!' cried Mrs Pepperpot, jumping up. 'In return you can promise to take me to the bonfire party tomorrow night and watch the

fireworks!'

So Mr Pepperpot promised and early next morning Mrs Pepperpot went to the store with her pockets full of one, two, five and ten-penny pieces.

'I want the pipe with the silver band on it,' said Mrs Pepperpot, when it was her turn to be served.

'Oh, what a shame,' said the grocer. 'I sold it to Joe Baker yesterday.'

'Well then, I shall have to hurry,' said Mrs Pepperpot and the bell clanged as she rushed out of the door.

She took the shortest way to Joe Baker's house, but only Mrs Baker was at home.

'I was wondering if Joe would sell me the pipe

he bought yesterday? I'll pay him good money for it,' said Mrs Pepperpot, making her full pockets clink.

'That pipe is no longer in the house,' said Mrs Baker. 'Do you think I want tobacco smoke in my curtains? No, thank you! I gave the pipe to some boy who was going to have a sale to get money to buy fireworks for the Midsummer's Eve party.'

'Tell me where the sale is!' yelled Mrs Pepperpot.

'Somewhere up on Windy Ridge,' said Mrs Baker.

18

'Then I must fly up there like the wind!' said Mrs Pepperpot, rushing off. But it was a long way to Windy Ridge and when Mrs Pepperpot arrived the sale was over. The boys were gathering up the paper and string and cardboard boxes and the bits that were left over to take up the hill to add to the bonfire.

'Who bought the pipe?' panted Mrs Pepperpot, so out of breath that her tongue was hanging out of her mouth.

'Pipe?' said the biggest boy.

'Yes, that nice big pipe with the silver band,' said Mrs Pepperpot.

'Oh that,' said the boy. 'My brother bought it, but then the silly ass tried to smoke it and got so sick that he tied it to a stick right on top of the bonfire.'

'Couldn't you take it down again?' said Mrs Pepperpot.

'Are you crazy?' said the boy. 'We're not going to spoil that lovely bonfire when we've got everything piled up so well. If anyone touches it everything will tumble down. No, we're going to have some fun with the pipe.

'But I've no time to talk to you now, I've got to go home and get some matches to light the bonfire.'

'Oh dear, oh dear,' wailed Mrs Pepperpot. 'There's nothing for it but to climb the bonfire myself and see if I can get the pipe down. I don't expect there will be anyone there yet.'

She was right, there was no one there, but the bonfire had been piled very high indeed, with old mattresses, one-legged chairs, bits of old fencing, worn-out clothes, old hats, car tyres and empty cartons. And right at the top of the bonfire was the pipe, tied firmly to a stick.

I shall have to try to knock it down, thought Mrs Pepperpot, but at that very moment she shrank – and for once Mrs Pepperpot was really pleased.

'Hurrah!' she said. 'It won't take long now for a little woman the size of a pepperpot to get the pipe down without upsetting the bonfire.'

Quick as a mouse Mrs Pepperpot darted into the big pile and started to climb. But it was not easy; as she crawled across a mattress, she got her heel stuck in a bed spring and took quite a time to free herself. Then she had difficulty in climbing a slippery chair-leg; she kept sliding back time after time, but at last she managed it.

After that she got entangled in the lining of a coat and groped about in the dark for some time before making her way out again. By this time

people had started to gather round the bonfire.

All right, thought Mrs Pepperpot, luckily I'm so small that they won't see me, and I'm going to get to the top, no matter what!

At that moment Mrs Pepperpot tumbled into a deep drawer and lay there puffing until she managed to catch hold of a bonnet string just above it and pull herself up.

'Thank goodness, there's not much further to go now,' said Mrs Pepperpot, but when she looked down she almost fainted. She had had no idea how high the bonfire was and now there were crowds of people waiting for it to be lit.

No time to lose, thought Mrs Pepperpot, heaving herself on to the last obstacle. This was easy, because it was an old concertina, so she could walk up it like a staircase.

Now she was at the foot of the stick and at the top was the pipe, securely tied.

However am I going to get up there? she thought, but then she noticed the edge of an empty tar barrel right next to her. So she smeared a little tar on her hands to give them a better grip and started to climb up the stick.

The bonfire shifted a little and the stick began to lean to one side and when she looked down she nearly died of fright: *the boys had lit the bonfire!*

Little flames were licking up round the mattresses and the broken chairs, the people were
cheering and the children were shrieking:

'Wait till it gets to the stick on top!'

I don't know why that should be such fun,
thought Mrs Pepperpot.

In any case I shall have to hurry to reach the
pipe.

And up she went, until she was clinging to the
pipe-stem with both hands.

'It won't be long before the fire gets to the
stick; then we'll see some fireworks!' shouted
the children. 'We've tied a rocket to the stick!'

'Oh dear oh dear oh dear,' said Mrs Pepperpot, hanging on tight, and at that moment there
was a bang and Mrs Pepperpot and the pipe and
the stick and the rocket shot up towards the red,
sunset sky.

But suddenly everyone stopped shouting.

'I thought I saw someone sitting on that stick,'
said a thin lady in a shawl.

'It looked like a little doll,' said an even
thinner lady who was wearing two shawls.

'Oh no, it couldn't be her, could it?' said
someone just behind the two ladies. It was Mr
Pepperpot, who had just left work and climbed

23

the hill to look at the bonfire. Now he swung himself on to his bicycle and raced home as fast as he could go.

'Oh, I hope you're at home, I hope you're at home,' he said, and when he opened the door his hands were shaking.

There stood Mrs Pepperpot in the kitchen, decorating his birthday cake, and on the table lay the pipe with the silver band.

'Many happy returns,' said Mrs Pepperpot. 'Come and eat now and afterwards you can put on a clean shirt and we'll go and dance round the bonfire together!'

The ladybird and the four wishes

Once upon a time there was a little old woman – no, what am I saying? She was a little girl. But this little girl worked every bit as hard as any grown woman. She wore a scarf round her head like a grown woman and she could weed a field of turnips like a grown woman and if any of the big boys started throwing lumps of earth at her, the little girl straightened up and told them off in a way that any grown woman would have been proud of.

When the little girl, whose name was Betsy, was weeding in the field one day, a ladybird came and settled on her thumb.

'What's this, you poor little thing, what are you doing on my thumb?' said Betsy. 'I can make a wish as long as you don't fly away. I'm going to make a wish!'

For, ever since she was very small, Betsy had been told to make a wish when a ladybird flew on to her finger.

'I wish, I wish... I had a new, red skipping-rope to use all the way to school and back!' said Betsy quickly, but then she remembered that she had borrowed a skipping-rope from her friend Anna, and lost it, so if Betsy got a new skipping-rope, she would have to give it to Anna.

'Just a minute, little ladybird, sit still, sit still, sit still!'

The ladybird crawled slowly right to the top of Betsy's thumb nail and she was so frightened that it would fly away that she scarcely dared to breathe. There were so many other things she wanted more than that silly old skipping-rope.

The ladybird turned round once or twice on the tip of her thumb before starting to crawl down the other side and up her first finger.

'Oh, now I wish, I wish... I could have some money!' said the little girl, but as soon as she had said it she was sorry, because she knew that she would be getting some money as soon as she had finished weeding the turnips. And in any case that would have to go to Mrs Mills to pay for the old bicycle she had bought from her.

The ladybird crawled right to the tip of Betsy's first finger, and began to raise and lower her shiny wing cases. Betsy was terrified that she would fly away, but the ladybird changed her mind and crawled down to the bottom of her first finger and up the hill again to the top of her middle finger.

Oh, now I must make a really good wish, and I must hurry, thought Betsy. Shall I wish to be a real princess – oh how silly of me, nobody could suddenly be a princess – no, I wish my mother will have no rheumatism in her back when I get home tonight!

This time Betsy felt she had made a good wish, because when her mother's rheumatism was painful, Betsy had to wash and feed her little brothers and sisters and put them to bed. If her mother did not have rheumatism in her back, Betsy would have time to play a little before she went to bed.

The ladybird crawled over the top of Betsy's middle finger and started to climb straight down into the gap before her third finger. But now the ladybird seemed to be tired, and did not look as if she wanted to fly away. She crawled very, very slowly up Betsy's third finger and Betsy tried to hurry her up a little with her other thumb, but that made the ladybird stand quite still and refuse to go on climbing for a long time. At last she reached the top of Betsy's third finger.

'I wish my father would get the job he went for today,' said Betsy. Her father had told her that if he got the job he would buy her a picture-book on his way home. But the ladybird sat quite still on the tip of her finger and suddenly she pulled her legs up under her and rolled off on to the ground. That would not do at all. The ladybird had to fly away with the wish to make it work.

Betsy lay down and put her little finger in front of the ladybird, but the little creature lay quite still. Finally Betsy had to pick her up very carefully and place her on her little finger. The ladybird did not move and Betsy began to feel very worried.

'Have I squeezed you so hard that you can't move? Can't you fly any more? Oh I'm so sorry, poor ladybird. Do be kind and fly, fly, fly!'

And suddenly the ladybird flew away, straight

towards the sun.

And now you shall hear something wonderful: when Betsy got home that night her mother's back was better than it had been for a long time, and her father had got the job he wanted, so Betsy had her picture-book. And Anna had come round to see her; she had found the old skipping-rope and had been given a new one, too, so now Betsy could have the old one. And Mrs Mills had been down to say that if Betsy would look after her little boy for a few hours, there would be nothing more to pay on the bicycle.

That must have been the luckiest ladybird ever!

Mr Learn-a-lot and the Singing Midges

One warm summer night Mrs Midge said to her daughters, 'Come along, girls, we're going to see Mr Learn-a-lot, the schoolmaster.'

'Is it a long way, Mama?' asked Big Sister Midge.

'Why are we going to see him, Mama?' said Middle Sister Midge.

'What are we going to do there, Mama?' said Little Midge.

'I thought we would sing something for him,' said Mother Midge. 'You have all learned to sing so well this summer that it's a pleasure to hear you, and Mr Learn-a-lot, is very interested in singing.'

So they flew off over the treetops and down to the house by the school where the teacher lived. Outside the bedroom they rested on the glass.

'Is the window shut, Mama?'

'Shan't we be able to get in, Mama?'

'Why doesn't he open the window, Mama?'

'Oh he'll open the window when he's going to bed,' said Mother Midge.

Soon afterwards the teacher opened the window.

'He's opened the window now, Mama.'

'Can't we go in now, Mama?'

'What shall we sing when we get inside, Mama?'

'Don't be so impatient now, there's no hurry. Mr Learn-a-lot needs time to take his clothes off first.'

'He's taken his clothes off, Mama!'

'So we can go *now*, Mama!'

'What if he goes to sleep before he's heard how well we sing, Mama?'

'It doesn't matter at all, he'll wake up soon enough when he hears us singing. I think you had better begin, Big Sister Midge.'

'What shall I sing for him, Mama?'

'You can sing *Merry Little Midges We*,' said Mother Midge, settling down behind the curtain with her other daughters. 'But you must remember to fly round his head in a circle and if he likes your singing he will sit up in bed. Off you go!'

And Big Sister Midge flew round in a circle over Mr Learn-a-lot's head, singing:

> Merry little midges we
> Praising summer sunshine bright;
> Spinning, springing, full of glee,
> Singing songs with all our might.
> On summer evenings warm and long,
> Hear the midges' whining song,
> Over meadows wide and long...
>   Let us have a bite!

Big Sister Midge sang the same verse three times over and was just beginning to believe that Mr Learn-a-lot did not like her song when he suddenly turned over and sat bolt upright in bed.

'Come back, come back!' urged Mother Midge.

'Wasn't I good, Mama?'

'Oh yes, you were very good. Now we'll wait a little while until the teacher is lying down again and then it will be Middle Sister Midge's turn, and she can sing *All of us will soon...*, which is a pretty song, and very suitable for the evening. Yes, now I think you can start, Middle Sister Midge. But you must not stop until Mr Learn-a-lot has jumped right out of bed and is standing in the middle of the floor. And you can fly a little lower than Big Sister Midge this time. Off you go!'

So Middle Sister Midge flew round and round in a circle, singing:

All of us will soon be grown-up midges,
We can go a-whistling, whee-ee, whee!
Dance where water flows and under bridges,
Playing 'Catch' and laughing, tee-hee-hee!

Middle Sister Midge had scarcely sung the first verse when Mr Learn-a-lot threw off his bed-clothes and leaped out of bed.

'Come back, come back!' urged Mother Midge.

'Well, talk about being good, *I* was jolly good, wasn't I?' said Middle Sister Midge, feeling very proud of herself.

'Now, now,' said Mother Midge, 'we midges never brag. Now it is Little Midge's turn.'

'What am I going to sing, Mama?' said Little Midge, who had the thinnest little voice you ever heard.

'You shall sing *The Midges' Lullaby*,' said Mother Midge solemnly, stroking Little Midge's transparent wings. 'It goes like this:

When the days are hot and slow,
The evening's cool and still.
Safe and happy that I know,
And I can drink my fill.

'Oh yes, I know that one,' said Little Midge, very pleased that her mother had chosen one of her favourites.

'And that will be our last song for tonight,' said Mother Midge, 'and you mustn't worry if you don't get a chance to sing the whole song. As soon as Mr Learn-a-lot begins to clap his hands you must stop and fly back to me as quickly and quietly as possible.'

Off flew Little Midge. Mr Learn-a-lot was lying quite still.

Little Midge sang:

When the days are hot and slow,
The evening's . . .

Clap! went Mr Learn-a-lot.

'Come back, come back!' said Mother Midge.

But Little Midge did not come back.

'Oh, dear sweet Little Midge, come back, come back!' piped Mother Midge, her voice shaking. And Little Midge came back.

'Why didn't you come right away?' said Mother Midge sternly.

'You told me to fly very quietly, Mama,' said Little Midge. 'Did I sing well, Mama?'

'Yes, yes, yes,' said Mother Midge. 'All of you were very good indeed, but now I want to ask you a question. What did you think of Mr Learn-a-lot?'

'He sat up in bed for the one who sang the longest,' said Big Sister Midge.

'He got out of bed for the one who sang the prettiest,' said Middle Sister Midge.

'He clapped his hands for the one who sang the highest,' said Little Midge.

'Yes, yes,' said Mother Midge. 'That is all well and good, but now I'm going to tell you what Mr Learn-a-lot really is. He is a good person. Shall we go and have a snack?'

'Yes!' sang the Midge daughters, and off they went to do as their mother told them.

Mrs Pepperpot learns to swim

As you know, Mrs Pepperpot can do almost anything, but until this summer there was one thing she couldn't do: she couldn't swim! Now I'll tell you how she learned.

When Mrs Pepperpot goes to the store she takes the short cut through a little wood, where there is a stream. At one point the stream widens out and turns into a pool, and in the pool the children play and splash and learn to swim. They haven't got a swimming teacher but the big ones teach the little ones. It's quite hard work sometimes and when they get bored the big ones who have to spend their time teaching the little ones say, 'If only we had a swimming teacher!'

'Much too expensive,' say the others. 'No, we'll have to go on teaching the small fry as best we can. It's a good thing the pool is not too deep so no one drowns when they get a little water in their ears.'

Then they also do 'dry exercises' on land. They lie on their tummies over a tree stump, kicking out with their arms and legs.

Mrs Pepperpot always stopped to watch them. 'If only I could do that!' she would say to herself.

Then the little ones learn something called 'the crawl'. 'We want to do the crawl, we want to do the crawl,' they shout, and they kick out backwards with their legs, and their arms whirl like windmills.

Oh, what fun it would be if I could do that too, thought Mrs Pepperpot, watching them as

usual, but she had nowhere to practise. True, she had tried it out in the kitchen once or twice. The first time she lay across a stool and began her 'dry swimming' with the basic movements, but just then her neighbour came round to borrow a cup of flour, and the second time, when she was going to 'crawl', she knocked over the soup that was cooking for her husband's supper and the whole lot poured all over her back.

But at night Mrs Pepperpot dreamed that she could swim – oh, how beautifully she swam! First she did the breast stroke, stretching out her arms, bending her knees, and then BANG! she gave the wall a great kick.

'What on earth is the matter with you now?' said Mr Pepperpot. 'Can't you let me sleep?' The way Mrs Pepperpot was kicking and carrying on had woken him up too.

'I'm swimming,' said Mrs Pepperpot.

'You're not swimming, you're dreaming,' said

her husband. 'And now be quiet!'

But soon afterwards Mrs Pepperpot was dreaming again and this time she was swimming on her back. The flowers standing on the window sill beside the bed were in great danger, but somehow they survived. 'And now I'm going to make some really strong strokes with my arms,' dreamed Mrs Pepperpot, striking out and hitting her husband on the nose.

'What are you up to now?' demanded Mr Pepperpot.

'I'm taking long, smooth strokes,' said Mrs Pepperpot, hitting her husband on the nose once more.

But it was still worse when she practised the crawl.

She pushed her way right down to the bottom

of the bed and shot forward from there, kicking her husband out of bed so that he landed on the floor with a crash. By now Mr Pepperpot was really angry. He picked up his bedcovers and shouted that if Mrs Pepperpot had to learn to swim she must find some water to swim in and a swimming teacher who could teach her how.

'Too expensive,' said Mrs Pepperpot. 'I'm learning from the children who bathe in the pool. One evening when there's no one there I want to go and see if I can really do it.'

'Well do that then!' said her husband crossly. 'But now I want to go to sleep and I shall sleep on the kitchen floor if you're going to practise any more strokes!'

'Well . . . I have heard there's something they call a swallow dive,' said Mrs Pepperpot.

'Oh help!' said her husband, and he shut the kitchen door.

But just after he had settled down in the kitchen he heard another CRASH! Mr Pepperpot sprang up and ran into the bedroom. There was his wife on the floor beside the bed with a big lump on her forehead.

'I tried the swallow dive, you see,' she said, rubbing the top of her head. 'But I suppose I didn't do it right.'

'No, that's obvious,' said Mr Pepperpot, thinking that he ought to shake his wife a little and get angry, but then he thought that if he got really angry he would have nothing but dry bread for breakfast and cold potatoes for dinner.

So all he said was, 'Tut tut tut!' and he scratched the back of his neck and went to bed.

One day the weather was fine and all the village children were going for a picnic in the mountains. Hurrah! thought Mrs Pepperpot. 'Now there will be no one in the pool so I shall go and try out my swimming.'

And so she did. When she reached the pool there was no one bathing, in fact there was no one to be seen anywhere.

'Well, it's not dangerous here, I heard the children say so,' said Mrs Pepperpot. 'I'm going to try a few swimming strokes for myself; it's not too deep here.'

'Here I go!' she said and in she jumped. But at that very moment she shrank to the size of a pepperpot! And now, of course, the little pool

seemed as big as the Atlantic Ocean.

'Help, help!' screamed Mrs Pepperpot. 'I'm drowning, I'm drowning!'

'Hold on, swimming teacher's coming,' said a voice from the bottom of the pool and up popped a big frog just where Mrs Pepperpot was splashing about. The clever frog somehow managed to get Mrs Pepperpot on his back.

'Oh, you really are a good swimmer,' said Mrs Pepperpot.

'I'm the best swimming teacher in the world,' replied the frog.

'Do you think you could teach me to swim?' said Mrs Pepperpot.

'Certainly. What would you like to learn?'

'First of all I'd like to learn the breast stroke,' said Mrs Pepperpot.

'That's all right, it's very simple. Just climb on my back, hold on tight, and watch how I kick out with my back legs.'

When the frog swam he moved his back legs so beautifully that Mrs Pepperpot learned the stroke almost at once.

'And then I thought I'd like to learn to swim on my back,' said Mrs Pepperpot.

'Ah, for that you had better talk to my children, the little tadpoles twirling round and round every which way down there in the water,' said the frog.

'Oh, I could never manage that,' said Mrs Pepperpot, when she saw how skilfully the tadpoles swam.

'Try it, try it,' said the tadpoles.

'Yes, yes, I'll give it a try,' said Mrs Pepperpot – and after a time she could swim on her back as well as anyone.

'And now I want to learn to do the crawl,' said Mrs Pepperpot, who was feeling really pleased with herself because she thought she could swim so well.

'We can teach you to do the crawl too,' said the tadpoles, and they twisted and turned in the water. Mrs Pepperpot tried to copy them – and after she had practised for a time she could even do that too.

'Right then, there is only the swallow dive left to learn,' said the frog. 'You will have to swim ashore and dive off that stone and I shall dive ahead of you.'

'Oooh, it's a bit deep here,' said Mrs Pepperpot.

'It has to be deep when you're doing a swallow dive, otherwise you'll bump your head,' said the frog. 'Watch me now, I'll dive first and then you follow.'

The frog dived. Mrs Pepperpot counted to three, gathered herself together and jumped, but at the very moment when she was flying through the air she grew to her usual size again.

SPLASH! and there was Mrs Pepperpot, rolling about in the little pool.

The frog had gone and the tadpoles had gone and Mrs Pepperpot looked round quickly to see if anyone had spotted her, but luckily there was nobody about.

She hurried home, changed into dry clothes and began to cook her husband's dinner – his favourite macaroni cheese.

The next evening, when the children had gone

home, Mrs Pepperpot went down to the pool and practised.

And she really could swim. A little bit, anyway.

'And if you can do a little, you can learn more,' said Mrs Pepperpot, winking in the direction of the little stone where she had taken off for her swallow dive. For under it sat the frog, with all the tadpoles swimming round him.

Four little kittens

Once upon a time there were four little kittens who were born in a barn.

'I really wonder what you will be when you grow up,' said the mother cat, licking the new-born kittens. They were very tiny and could not even see yet. They could only mew in piping voices and creep close to their mother.

After a few days the kittens could see and every day they grew bigger and stronger. And rowdier, thought the mother cat, when the kittens clambered on her back and bit her tail.

'Now listen to me,' said the mother cat one day. 'You are all so big now that you must decide what kind of cats you are going to be.'

'Tell us what kind of cats we can be,' mewed the kittens. 'Tell us about all the kinds of cats there are, so that we can decide for ourselves!' And the mother cat sat down and half-closed her green eyes.

'There's something they call the alley cat. An alley cat is long, with a flexible back. He steals through any garden fence, sleeps where it suits him and takes food where he finds it.

'Uncle Harry is an alley cat. He has lots of friends and they hold beautiful concerts when the moon is bright.

'He has enemies too – dogs, car wheels and rainy gutters where he get his paws wet. But a genuine alley cat is never afraid!'

'That would suit me,' said Ruff, the biggest kitten, and off he went to be an alley cat like Uncle Harry.

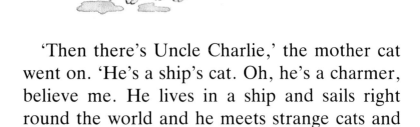

'Then there's Uncle Charlie,' the mother cat went on. 'He's a ship's cat. Oh, he's a charmer, believe me. He lives in a ship and sails right round the world and he meets strange cats and hunts the foreign rats.

'A ship's cat becomes a world traveller, and he is brave and cheerful. Uncle Charlie knows plenty of beautiful sailor songs, I can tell you.'

'That's for me,' said Tuff, the second kitten, and off he went to become a ship's cat like Uncle Charlie.

'Then there's the barn cat,' the mother cat went on.

'That's what I am – a barn cat. I catch mice and hunt rats while the farmer is asleep at night. I live in the barn and sleep on a sack behind the water-butt, as you know.

'A barn cat is good friends with all the animals on the farm. We make ourselves useful, if I say so myself.'

'I want to be like you, Mother,' said the third kitten, whose name was Miaow. And off she went to become a barn cat just like her mother.

And the mother cat purred with pleasure over her three eldest kittens.

Now there was only the last and littlest kitten left. Her name was Pussypuss. Pussypuss was playful and kind and kept her paws clean.

The mother cat sighed. 'Dear Pussypuss, I don't think it would suit you to be an alley cat or a ship's cat or a barn cat. I'm afraid you will have to find something for yourself.'

And the mother cat went off to catch mice.

Poor Pussypuss felt very miserable as she went off to find out what she was going to be.

First she saw Miaow, who was biting a big rat in the back of the neck.

'Ugh no, I'm not going to be a barn cat,' she said. 'I don't want to catch rats.'

Pussypuss walked on until she came to the town. In a backyard she met Ruff, who was spitting at a puppy.

'Wuff, wuff,' barked the puppy, but Ruff put up his back and stuck his tail in the air like a brush and the puppy ran away.

So did Pussypuss.

She ran down to the shore and there she caught sight of Tuff, high up on the mast of a big ship. The sailors were stowing ropes and other things that had to be neat and tidy for the ship's departure, and they were singing:

Farewell, adieu my little friend,
I'm sailing far away.
And you, alas must stay behind
and miss me all
the day.

'Ooh, I wouldn't have dared to go with him for anything in the world,' said Pussypuss. 'But now I really must find out what kind of cat I am.'

Pussypuss walked on. It began to rain and the sky grew darker and darker and Pussypuss grew wetter and wetter.

When evening came she lay down on an old sack to sleep. *Then* . . . down came a huge hand and dropped Pussypuss into a pocket!

Pussypuss spat and clawed at first, but it was nice and warm in the pocket and soon she fell asleep.

When Pussypuss opened her eyes again she was inside a house which seemed to be filled with cushions and rugs and curtains. There was a good, hot stove too and there was also a little girl, with kind, gentle hands.

'Oh, what a sweet little kitten,' said the little girl. 'And I've been longing for a kitten all my life! Now I shan't have to be lonely any more.'

The little girl gave Pussypuss cream in a small bowl. Pussypuss drank it all up, keeping one paw in the bowl so that it should not tip up. Afterwards she washed her paws and whiskers. That had been much nicer than mouse to eat!

The little girl played with Pussypuss. She found some balls of wool and Pussypuss ran after them or tried to catch them. This was a good deal better than trudging along roads and getting wet paws!

The little girl took Pussypuss on to her lap and sang: 'My puss is my puss and no one else's puss.' Pussypuss purred comfortably. That was a much better song than the silly sailor song!

'Now I know what I'm going to be,' purred Pussypuss. 'Because now I know what kind of

cat I am. I'm a cat who likes cushions and cream.
And I like lying on a little girl's lap because she's
kind and strokes my back. I am a house cat!'

So all four kittens lived happily in their own
way. Ruff in the alley, because he was an alley
cat; Tuff on deck because he was a ship's cat;
Miaow in the barn because she was a barn cat;
and Pussypuss on a cushion in a house with a
little girl, because Pussypuss was a house cat.

Mr Pepperpot's bad mood

Things were not at all cheerful at Mrs Pepperpot's house. Mr Pepperpot was in a bad mood – he had been in it for days – and Mrs Pepperpot simply didn't know how to get him out of it. She put flowers on the table and cooked him his favourite dish, fried bacon with macaroni cheese, but it was no use: Mr Pepperpot just went on moping.

'I don't know what's the matter with him,' sighed Mrs Pepperpot. 'Perhaps he's pining for pancakes.' So she made him a big pile of pancakes.

When her husband came in for dinner his face lit up at the sight of them but as soon as he began to eat he became as glum as before.

'Ah well,' he sighed, staring up at the ceiling with sorrowful eyes, 'it doesn't really matter. . .'

'I've had enough of this sighing,' said Mrs Pepperpot. 'It's bad enough for you, having something on your mind, but it's no fun for me either, watching your face getting longer and longer every day. For a moment there you began to look cheerful again and I was so pleased because I thought it was just the pancakes you'd been missing.'

'Yes, you've got something there,' said her husband, 'but it's not only pancakes I've been missing, there's something else besides, you know.'

'Yes, but you must tell me what it is!' said Mrs Pepperpot.

'It's just the thought of a bit of blueberry jam on them for once, not pancakes all by themselves,' sighed Mr Pepperpot.

At last Mrs Pepperpot understood. She had not put any blueberry jam on her pancakes for many months.

'Well, if that's all you're making such a fuss about I'll go to the blueberry copse this very day and this very moment!' said Mrs Pepperpot, and snatching a pail which was hanging on the wall she set off at once.

She walked fast, as all women do when they are cross with their husbands, and soon she had reached the blueberry bushes. She put the pail down under a bush and began to pick, popping them into the cup she had in her apron pocket. All the time she was talking to herself.

'I've never seen such a stupid man as mine, bless my soul, wasn't it stupid of me to marry him, too, there's only one person sillier than I was then, and that's my husband, gracious me, what a silly man. There, now the cup's full and I must empty it into the pail.'

Cup after cup after cup was filled and the pail was filling up all the time until it needed only one more cupful. But just as she had filled the last cup she shrank to the size of a pepperpot!

'Well, now I am in a jam!' she said to herself, 'but I can probably manage to drag the little cup over to the pail if I push and pull hard enough.' So linking both arms through the handle, she began to pull the cup along. It was rather heavy at first, but then she reached an ant path made of slippery pine needles which made it much easier because the cup slid along over the needles. And all the time little ants and big ants scuttled to and fro.

'Good afternoon, ants,' said Mrs Pepperpot, 'so you're hard at work today too. Oh yes, there's always someone who has to push and someone to pull,' she said, but the ants were much too busy to talk to her.

'Can't you stop for a moment and have a chat?' she said. 'Oh well, I can talk to myself, that way I won't trouble anyone,' and with that she sat down and rested with her back against the cup.

While she was sitting there she suddenly felt someone breathing down her neck and when she turned round there was a fox grinning at her and waving his tail.

'Hallo, Mr Fox, are you taking a stroll?' said Mrs Pepperpot. 'It's lucky you don't know that my hens are – oh dear, I nearly let my tongue run away with me!'

'Do go on,' said the fox, in his silkiest voice.

'That would be telling, wouldn't it?' said Mrs Pepperpot. 'But as you see I've got a cup of blueberries here which I have to drag over to the pail by that bush and I haven't got time to talk to you.'

'If I carry your cup you'll be able to talk,' said the fox.

'Thanks very much,' said Mrs Pepperpot. 'Well, as I was saying, my hens – there now, my

tongue nearly ran away with me again!'

'Just go on talking, your tongue won't run away,' smirked the fox.

'No, I don't usually talk too much but some-how it's so easy to say that my hens are – there, I nearly said it. But we're there now, thank you so much, just put the cup down and I'll tell you.'

'Yes, tell me, I'm not going to take your hens,' said the fox.

'No you're not!' laughed Mrs Pepperpot. 'I've lent all my hens to the neighbours to hatch out their eggs.'

When the fox realized that he had been tricked he was so ashamed that he ran off into the thickest bushes and hid himself.

'Ha ha ha, that was a good trick you played on the fox!' said a voice very close to Mrs Pepper-pot, and when she turned round, there was the wolf.

'Well, good day to you, Mr Wolf!' said Mrs Pepperpot. 'What a good thing you came, you can help me to empty the cup into the pail.'

'Oh no, I'm not as easily tricked as that fox,' said the wolf.

'I wasn't thinking of tricking you,' said Mrs Pepperpot, 'but you'd better do as I say, or I'll send for One-eye Threadless.'

'I've heard about old wives' tales, but I've never heard that one before,' sniffed the wolf.

'It's not an old wives' tale,' said Mrs Pepperpot, 'and anyway I'm no ordinary old wife. You can see I'm as small as a pepperpot, and One-eye Threadless is my servant.'

'I'd like to see that servant of yours,' said the wolf.

'Well, if you just stick your nose in my apron

pocket, you can have a look at him,' said Mrs Pepperpot. So the wolf popped his nose in her apron pocket and pricked it on a sharp needle she had in there.

'Ouch!' shouted the wolf, and off he ran towards the forest, but Mrs Pepperpot called him back: 'Oh no, first you empty the cup into the pail, and don't you dare spill a single berry, otherwise I shall call One-eye Threadless to prick you again.'

The wolf didn't dare disobey her, but as soon as he had finished he shot off like an arrow in the same direction as the fox.

Mrs Pepperpot laughed as she watched him go, but then she heard something rustle near the pail, and this time it was the bear himself.

'Oh dear me, good day, dear me, dear me,' said Mrs Pepperpot in a small voice, curtseying so low she nearly disappeared in the bushes. 'Has the fine weather brought Your Majesty out for a walk?'

'Yes,' growled the bear, sniffing at the bucket.

'How fortunate for me! As Your Majesty can see, I've picked a whole bucketful of berries but it's not very safe for a little woman like me to walk about in the forest alone. Would Your Majesty be so kind as to carry my bucket as far as the road?'

'I don't know about that,' said the bear. 'I like blueberries myself.'

'Yes, of course,' said Mrs Pepperpot, 'but you're not like the rest of them, Your Majesty, you know how to control yourself, and you would always help a poor little woman like me.'

'No, I want some blueberries!' said the bear, lowering his head. In a flash Mrs Pepperpot was on his back, scratching him behind the ears.

'What are you up to?' asked the bear.

'I'm just giving you a little scratch behind the ears,' said Mrs Pepperpot. 'Doesn't it feel good?'

'Oh yes, it's almost better than blueberries,' growled the bear.

'Well, if Your Majesty would be so kind as to carry my pail into the road, I'll go on scratching Your Majesty's ears all the way.'

'All right, all right, I'll do it,' said the bear.

When they came to the edge of the road the bear placed the bucket carefully on a flat stone.

'Thank you, thank you very much indeed,' said Mrs Pepperpot.

'Thank *you*,' said the bear, shuffling off into the forest.

When the bear had gone Mrs Pepperpot grew back to her usual size, picked up the bucket and hurried home.

'It's no trouble looking after yourself when you're small, as long as you know how to deal with people you meet,' she said to herself. 'You have to trick the tricky ones, frighten the cowards and scratch the strong ones behind the ears.

'But there's only one thing you can do for gloomy husbands, and that's put blueberry jam on their pancakes!'